MYSTERY of the LOST LETTER

Written by Olive Blake

Illustrated by Sanford Kossin

Troll Associates

Troll Associates, Mahwah, N.J.

Library of Congress Catalog Card Number: 78-18037
ISBN 0-89375-093-X

"Do you have the letter?" asked Mrs. Banks.

"I have it," said Jane.

"Don't lose it," said her mother.

"I won't," said Jane.

"Remember," said her mother.

"No problem," said Jane.

"Do you have the money?" asked Mrs. Banks.

Jane held up the money.

"Don't lose it," said her mother.

"Don't worry," said Jane.

"Remember," said her mother.

"Mother!" cried Jane. "I will *not* lose the money. I will *not* lose the letter. I will go

straight to the post office. I will buy a stamp.
Then I will lick the stamp and paste it on the
envelope."

"And then?" asked Mrs. Banks.

"And then," said Jane, "I will mail the
letter."

"Good!" said Mrs. Banks. "After you mail the letter, you may go to the candy store and buy a treat for yourself."

Jane gave her mother a kiss.

"Goodbye," said Mrs. Banks. "And Jane dear, remember. It is a very important letter. Go straight to the post office. Do not stop on the way."

"I promise," said Jane. Then she hurried out the door, and started down the street to the post office.

On the way, Jane met her best friend, Suzy Brown. Suzy was carrying a cup of sugar.

"Where are you going?" Suzy asked.

"I am going to the post office to mail a very important letter," said Jane.

"I am going to return this cup of sugar to Mrs. Simon," said Suzy. "If you will come with me, I will go with you."

"I can't," said Jane. "I promised to go straight to the post office."

"It will only take a minute," said Suzy.

"All right," said Jane. "I suppose one minute will not matter."

Mrs. Simon thanked them for the sugar.

"Come in, girls," she said. "I just baked a fresh batch of brownies."

"I would really like to," said Jane, "but I am on my way to the post office with a very important letter."

"It will only take a minute," said Mrs. Simon.

"All right," said Jane. "I suppose one more minute will not matter."

Suzy ate three brownies. Jane ate two. They each had a glass of milk with a straw that could bend.

"Thank you for the brownies," said Jane and Suzy when it was time to go.

"You're welcome, girls," said Mrs. Simon. "Come again."

"After I mail the letter," said Jane to Suzy, "I am going to buy a piece of candy. You may have half."

"Let's buy the candy first," said Suzy.

"No," said Jane. "I have to go straight to the post office. I promised."

"It will only take a minute," said Suzy. "One little minute won't hurt."

"I guess you are right," said Jane. "What can happen in just one minute?"

"Let's get something chocolate," said Suzy.

"Something chewy," said Jane.

"Something with nuts," said Suzy.

"Something with coconut," said Jane.

"I have just the thing," said Mrs. Toddleberry. "It has chocolate and nuts and coconut."

"Is it chewy?" asked Jane.

"Would I forget chewy?" asked Mrs. Toddleberry. "It has chocolate. It has nuts. It has coconut. It is chewy."

"Perfect!" said Jane. And she bought the candy.

"Guess where we are going now?" said Jane to Suzy as they left the candy store.

"To the ice cream shop?" asked Suzy.

"To the post office!" said Jane.

"I would like one stamp, please," said Jane to the postal clerk. She put her money on the counter.

"Here you are, young lady," said the clerk.

"And now," said Jane to Suzy, "all I have to do is lick this stamp, paste it on the envelope, and mail my mother's letter."

"Well," said Suzy, "what are you waiting for?"

Jane was looking in her pockets.
"What is the matter?" asked Suzy.
Jane was crawling on the floor.
"What happened?" asked Suzy.

"I lost the letter!" said Jane.

"You didn't!" cried Suzy.

"I did," said Jane. "What am I going to do?"

"Think," said Suzy. "When did you have it last?"

"At Mrs. Simon's," said Jane. "I put it down when I ate the brownies."

"The case is solved," said Suzy. "The letter is on Mrs. Simon's kitchen table."

"It isn't," said Jane. "I just remembered. I took it with me when we left."

"Did you have it in the candy store?" asked Suzy.

"I can't remember," said Jane.

"Think!" said Suzy.

"I *am* thinking!" said Jane. "Now I remember. I put the letter on a pile of newspapers when I was taking out my money."

"Come on," said Suzy. "Hurry! It may still be there."

The letter was gone.

Mrs. Toddleberry was behind the counter. "Hello, again," she said. "What can I do for you?"

"I left a very important letter right

here," said Jane. "It's not here now. Do you happen to know where it is?"

"You left a very important letter on a pile of newspapers?" said Mrs. Toddleberry.

"It was only for a minute," said Jane.

"*Only* for a minute!" exclaimed Mrs. Toddleberry. "Do you know what can happen in a minute? A flower can open. A star can fall. A letter can be lost forever. That's what can happen in a minute."

Jane began to cry.

"There now," said Mrs. Toddleberry. "Tears don't solve anything."

"What am I going to do?" sniffed Jane.

"If I were you," said Mrs. Toddleberry, "I would look for a tall man in a blue raincoat."

"A tall man?" asked Suzy.

"In a blue raincoat?" asked Jane. "What has he got to do with my letter?"

"Maybe nothing," said Mrs. Toddleberry. "Maybe everything. He was here just a few minutes ago. He bought a newspaper from the top of that pile."

As Jane and Suzy were leaving, Mrs. Toddleberry called after them, "There is one more clue, girls. The man in the blue raincoat was carrying a pile of books."

"Thank you," said Jane.

"Good luck," said Mrs. Toddleberry.

"Someone tall," said Jane.

"Someone wearing a blue raincoat," said Suzy.

"Someone carrying a pile of books," said Jane.

"Where shall we look?" asked Suzy.

"Beats me," said Jane.

Jane and Suzy walked up the street. They walked quickly. They did not want the tall man in the blue raincoat to get away.

"Do you see him?" asked Jane.

"Not yet," said Suzy.

"Look!" cried Jane. "There he is!" She pointed across the street. "See that man? He is tall. He is wearing a blue raincoat. And he has a newspaper tucked under his arm!"

"I don't see any books," whispered Suzy.

"Maybe he lost them," said Jane.

"No," said the man. "I did not lose a pile of books."

"Are you sure?" asked Jane.

"Of course I am sure," said the man.

"What have you got hidden in that newspaper?" asked Suzy.

"What indeed!" said the man.

"It may be my letter," said Jane.

"Ridiculous!" snapped the man.

"It may be *stuck* in there," said Jane.

"Preposterous!" said the man.

Jane began to cry.

"There, there," said the man. "Don't do that." He opened his newspaper and shook it out. "See?" he said. "It is not there. I do not have your letter."

"I'm sorry," sniffed Jane.

"Tut, tut," said the man. He shook his head and walked away.

Jane and Suzy stopped every man who looked tall. Some were wearing raincoats. Some were carrying books. Some just looked suspicious. None of them had the letter.

"Let's try the library," said Suzy. "It is as good a place as any to look for a man with a pile of books."

"I don't see any blue raincoats," said Jane.

"Except for that one!" said Suzy. She

pointed to a raincoat hanging over the back
of an empty chair.

On a table, in front of the chair, was a
pile of books. Next to the books was a folded
newspaper. And on top of the newspaper
was a white envelope!

"My letter!" cried Jane. She ran to the letter and picked it up.

"Stop, thief!" screeched an excited little woman. "Put down that letter at once!"

Jane dropped the letter. "I'm sorry," she said. "I thought you were taller."

"I thought you were a man," said Suzy.

"We thought it was *my* letter," explained Jane.

"Quiet!" hissed a man. He stood up. He was very tall. He picked up a raincoat from the seat next to his. The raincoat was blue.

"A person can't find peace and quiet anyplace!" he complained loudly. He put on his raincoat.

Jane and Suzy watched as he picked up his books and his newspaper. They watched as an envelope fell out of the newspaper and fluttered to the floor.

"I can't believe I found it," said Jane.
She pulled down the handle of the mailbox,
and dropped the letter inside.

"See you tomorrow," said Suzy.
"See you," said Jane.

"I'm home!" called Jane. She opened the closet and hung up her jacket.

"What took you so long?" asked Mrs. Banks. "Did everything go all right? Did you mail my letter?"

"Of course," replied Jane. "What could go wrong?"